SHEILA WATSON was born in New Westminster, British Columbia, in 1909. She took her B.A. (1931) and M.A. (1933) from the University of British Columbia, and then taught in elementary and high schools on the B.C. mainland and on Vancouver Island before beginning further graduate studies in English literature at the University of Toronto after the Second World War.

In the early 1950s, Watson lived in Calgary, where she wrote much of her novel *The Double Hook*. In the same decade, she continued her graduate studies, working on Wyndham Lewis under the supervision of Marshall McLuhan.

In 1961 Watson joined the Department of English at the University of Alberta. With colleagues there, she was a founder and editor of *White Pelican*, an avant-garde journal of literature and the visual arts. She retired from teaching in 1975, and moved in 1980 to Nanaimo, British Columbia.

In 1992 she published *Deep Hollow Creek*, a novel she had written in the late 1930s.

Sheila Watson died in Nanaimo, British Columbia, in 1998.

Sheila Watson

A FATHER'S KINGDOM

The Complete Short Fiction

With an Afterword by Glenn Willmott

M&S

National Library of Canada Cataloguing in Publication

Watson, Sheila, 1909-1998
A father's kingdom : the complete short fiction / Sheila Watson ; afterword
by Glenn Willmott.

(New Canadian library)
Includes bibliographical references.
ISBN 0-7710-3488-1

I. Title.   II. Series.

PS8545.A88A159 2004   C813'.54   C2003-905997-9

We acknowledge the financial support of the Government of Canada
through the Book Publishing Industry Development Program and that of
the Government of Ontario through the Ontario Media Development
Corporation's Ontario Book Initiative. We further acknowledge the
support of the Canada Council for the Arts and the Ontario Arts Council
for our publishing program.

Typeset in Minion by M&S, Toronto
Printed and bound in Canada

McClelland & Stewart Ltd.
The Canadian Publishers
481 University Avenue
Toronto, Ontario
M5G 2E9
www.mcclelland.com/NCL

1 2 3 4 5   08 07 06 05 04

Contents

Acknowledgements

The stories in this collection originally appeared in the following publications:

"Rough Answer" *Canadian Forum* (September 1938).
"Brother Oedipus" *Queen's Quarterly* (Summer 1954).
"The Black Farm" *Queen's Quarterly* (Summer 1956).
"Antigone" *The Tamarack Review* (Spring 1959).
"The Rumble Seat" *Open Letter* (3:1, 1974).
"And the Four Animals" *Five Stories* (Toronto: Coach House Press, 1980).

A Father's Kingdom

Rough Answer

MARGARET STOOD at the door of the cabin. She watched the thin blue light of evening merge into the dark blue green of coming night. She heard the plaintive honking of some geese as they passed overhead, an arrow of blackness in the translucent sky. Somewhere in the black hills a coyote barked. "Joe will be coming soon," she thought. "The school lady will be tired."

She strained forward into the darkening evening, listening. The silence surged around her, cut off all contact with reality. The long drawn wail of the coyote wrenched her back to life. She went into the house and stirred up the fire. She lit the lamp. She looked once more into the little room which Joe had built by putting up a thin partition down the length of their one room. As she turned back to the fire she heard the rattle of wagon wheels coming over the culvert.

"Ho Major! Ho Colonel!" Joe's voice rang clear with laughter. "They couldn't hurt you nowise. We're here all right and Margaret'll make you comfortable."

Margaret went to the door with the lamp.

"Come in," she said. "Joe'll put the horses in and bring your things."

She watched Joe help the girl down from the high wagon. "She's pretty," she thought, "pretty like you don't see around here."

The girl pulled her fur jacket close about her and let Joe help her to the door.

"You must be cold," said Margaret, letting her eyes travel down the slim length of silk-clad leg, letting them rest for a moment on the queer strapped slippers. Her voice rang with a half suppressed note of disapproval.

"It's cold," the girl said with a slight shudder as she went into the house.

"Pretty," the girl thought to herself. "Pretty enough but old looking. I suppose they grow old living here – like this."

She felt a little frightened. She wouldn't let her thoughts rest on those months of boredom.

"God knows what I'll find to do," she thought.

Margaret took her into her bed-room. She lit a candle. The light flickered on the white spread, the work table and the frilled dresser.

"It looks like a hermit's cell," thought the girl.

"I hope you'll be comfortable," said Margaret. "Ask for anything you want. I'll give you warm water and Joe he'll fetch you a tubful Friday nights."

Good heavens! the girl hadn't thought of that. "In these places they didn't bathe, did they?" She had known that before. She was just beginning to realize, though, what she'd done. She could stick it anyway if things didn't pall too much. Joe – that was the man's name, wasn't it? – had asked her if she could ride. She had lied about it. Said she loved it. Perhaps he'd take her out sometime. He wasn't bad looking in his own way. A little rough – but then – he'd be much more amusing than Margaret. "She looks," the girl's thoughts hesitated – "she looks good."

At supper Joe seemed to be in a very good humour. He told several stories. Joe didn't talk much as a rule. When he spoke it was of the price of beef or irrigating or fencing or of the new corral he was going to build.

"Trying to cheer the girl up," thought Margaret. She, too, spoke more than was her wont. She and Joe didn't need to speak much. They knew. A third person changed things somehow. Broke the contact. Silence seemed a little shameless, a little naked.

"They're right glad to have a lady teacher," she said. "We've had men so long. It'll be nice to have a woman about."

"I'll let you have the bay mare to ride," said Joe. "Then you can come and go as you like. Margaret'll show you round."

The girl's eyelids fluttered slightly. She hadn't thought of that. Margaret would ride. Ride with Margaret – she might have saved herself the trouble of a lie.

"You must be tired," said Margaret. "Joe'll take you to school in the morning to get you acquainted with the way."

The girl went into her room. She felt a little depressed, a long way from nowhere. She shut the flimsy door and opening the window, lit a cigarette.

"The man's rather nice looking," she thought. She yawned and stared out into the darkness.

Margaret and Joe looked at each other.

"She's pretty," said Margaret, "but I think she'll find it quiet here."

"Don't know," said Joe. He felt a little disturbed. He'd never felt that way before, not that he could remember. He couldn't just say. He felt he should say something. He didn't know what. A third person always made a difference he guessed. He began to whistle under his breath.

The week hadn't been so bad, thought the girl on Friday night as she sat curled round in the corrugated tub of warm water which Joe had fetched for her. She was getting used to things. She dried herself and slipped into a thin white dress which showed the curves of her slim body. She sat down on the bed and polished her nails.

"Margaret's a funny woman," she thought. "Cuts her nails straight across as if she didn't care." Joe noticed those things, too. She was conscious of his eyes following her sometimes. Her thoughts hurried on, slipping over things she wouldn't really think about. "He's really nice," she thought, "not the kind of man . . ." She rose abruptly and, putting on a sweater, went out.

Margaret was peeling the vegetables for supper.

"Going to watch Joe feed?" she asked. "He's going to

take you up to see the critters tomorrow. Thought you'd like to tell them at home about it, he did. We don't want you to be lonely like."

"That will be nice. I can write them a long letter." The girl went out and down towards the yard.

Margaret went into her room and opened the window. She didn't like the smell of smoke. She went back and began to cut the turnips into squares. She set the table, putting a side plate and napkin for the girl.

"I suppose she's different to me, that's all," she thought. "Her way's not my ways."

She felt resentment rising in her throat. Her silence had been shattered. The presence of the girl in the house rang through the silence, the vibrant reality which was her only refuge, the tacit understanding she had with life. She couldn't have explained it, but she knew.

Joe was different too. He sang sometimes and talked, as if to clothe the silence which had been theirs, the understanding which they had arrived at without words the first night she had come home with him.

Joe looked up. He saw the girl coming. "Slim and white like them lilies on the mountain," he thought. Then he checked himself. He was thinking too much about that girl, he was, the way she moved, the helpless look in her eyes when she asked him to do anything, the soft white skin disappearing down her dress at the back of her neck. He didn't think of Margaret like that. She was a fact, was Margaret, a mighty pleasant fact, too, with her long, unbroken silence and her quiet ways; but still, a man – he liked the flowers, didn't he? – sort of made your throat ache to see them standing straight, their cups filled with sunlight.

The girl came up to him as he tossed down the hay. "You seem busy," she said. "It's nice out here." She leant against the bars of the fence. Joe tossed down more hay. He began to whistle. She leant there, looking up the hill lonesome like. He saw the sunlight glint on her pale hair. His hand ached to touch the soft skin at her throat. "Wonder what it would feel like," he thought, "soft and warm like a horse's nostrils." But he shouldn't think that way. He knew that.

"He seems queer," thought the girl. "Don't think he'll ever be the real thing." She thought of the stories she had read – silent men, strong and passionate. Her own experience had not led her beyond the college boy type. She felt lonesome again. She was definitely bored but slightly expectant.

The next day Joe saddled the mare and his own fancy-looking stud. He felt himself possessed by a new sort of vanity, a desire to look smart. He had shaved and put on a clean shirt. Margaret had lent the girl a pair of over-alls and Joe buckled her into his chaps.

"It'll be windy there," he said, bending closer as he tugged at the buckle, close enough to catch her fragrant warmth.

The mare was gentle but he went slowly. Anyone with half an eye in his head could see that the girl couldn't ride. Margaret sat a horse well. Rode like a man.

It gave Joe a protective feeling, a feeling twin brother to his new vanity to see her sitting slim and helpless on the mare. She bumped up and down in the saddle.

"Press yourself against the cantle," he suggested. "You'll ride easier."

When they reached the top of the hill the girl looked uncomfortably tired.

"Let's rest for a bit," he suggested. He knew he shouldn't suggest it. He felt that his feet were on marshy ground. His feeling of vanity was oozing away, but the protective feeling became stronger.

"It's a long way, isn't it," she said. He helped her down from the mare. Her hair brushed across his mouth. He let his hand rest on her shoulder for a moment. He wouldn't – not he, but the next moment she had let her head slip forward on his shoulder.

"I'm so tired." Her voice had a plaintive ring.

"We could go back," he said, knowing that he should go back at once. Margaret was his woman. The girl moved a little closer.

"I'm so lonely," she said, and began to whimper a little.

Joe knew what he should do – what you did to mares when they get a little skittish. He knew, but he stood gazing over the level stretch of the range. He thought of Margaret.

"You do tempt a man to pity," he said, "like young mares in the spring or yearling heifers."

She sprang back as if struck, her face crimson.

"How could you say that," she cried out. She felt perhaps it was true, but she wouldn't think, not for anything. He was crude, crude beyond belief.

"Let's go – back," she said.

He helped her to mount. He felt indifferent now. He looked out to where the blue sky and the yellow hills met. He felt the power of their silence.

That night the girl spoke to Margaret.

"I'm going," she said. "It's lonesome here. I shouldn't have come. I'm not made your way."

She wanted desperately to think. Joe had wakened in her a feeling, a stirring of realization which she could not comprehend. She felt different towards Margaret somehow. Yet she wanted to go. She wasn't ready to meet herself yet.

The next morning Joe drove her to the station.

"They'll have to get another girl for the school," Margaret said.

"I think they'll get a man again," said Joe.

They sat down to supper. Margaret's thoughts moved slowly. Joe's my man, she thought. He's life. Like rain for plants or hay for critters. The girl's gone. She thought of the slim length of the girl's supple legs.

"Beef's gone up," said Joe. "They told me at the station."

The light flickered on the plates. Margaret rose and stirred the fire. She felt at peace once more.

"We won't board no more school-teachers," said Joe.

"No," said Margaret.

A coyote howled in the hills. The dog barked. They did not notice it. They sat each wrapped in his own thoughts, their silence unbroken.

Brother Oedipus

OUR BROTHER'S name was Oedipus. Perhaps our father, who was a doctor, chose the name in some moment of illumination as he snipped and sewed together fragments of human life. Perhaps he chose it during his long hours of consultation. He did not say. Our mother gave no reason for anything she did. We contented ourselves with learning to pronounce the name; and, as children will, we called him Old Puss and sometimes in more playful mood Puss-Puss or Boots.

Of all of us Oedipus was most attached to our mother. He was always at odds with her, of course, since he could not ignore her. Indeed none of us ignored her completely for as children she dominated our lives. A small woman, tough and robust, she conditioned what our father had begotten since his occupation confined him to the more difficult work of reconditioning nature at large. Living under her discipline, I felt her restrictive, and would never have considered comparing her to the sea or to the earth as poets compare these free vague symbols to a

mother. As I grew older, had I been tempted to meta-
phor, I should have seen her not as something large and
formless like the poet's earth, but as something simple
and arbitrarily precise as a cartographer's image of it:
Yellow as the map of China, criss-crossed with isobars.
Oedipus's mind was of different texture.

One night he called me out under his willow tree.

"See," he said. He had scrawled a few lines on the
back of a telephone bill.

> *I have often heard her say she gave me suck*
> *And it should seem by that she dearly loved me*
> *Since Princes seldom do it.*

Puss said, "When you read the Elizabethans you always
get what you want and you aren't always detected."

"When I was young," I said, "I would have blushed to
read those lines. The breast was a thing of naught, meta-
physically and physically."

"I have always been self-conscious," said Puss, "but I
have solved the problem of relationships. I have gone
back to the elemental womb, tomb – cave, grave. I have
taken refuge in the arched earth cave."

Could we, I wondered, be thinking of the same thing?

I looked at Puss. His eyes were on the willow.

Our mother was neat and well-shaped – flat, and
tight, and leathery.

The branches of the willow seemed to shut us off
from a world of honking cars and cycling children.

"It is only here I have peace," said Oedipus. He looked at the branches yellow-curving to the earth.

"One could sit under the branches," he said, "in a golden summer-house, but this is a romantic's dream. I must dig deep to find peace."

"If you grasp the willow," I said, "it might come away like Persephone's shrub. You would have your cave; the thing is probably rooted in hell."

"I rather suspect," he said, "that it is rooted in our mother's drain."

At that very moment our mother was looking out of her window. She observed what passed in the world or all of it that mattered. She watched Oedipus's comings and goings and noted the movements of his wife.

"Much as I admire the old lady," Oedipus said, "I resent the housing tension that has confined us to the same block. There is in the hierarchy of fates a lesser deity which might be called Nuisance."

He took me off to show me his roses. He fed them capsules every day and brooded over them.

"It is not the fashion," he said, "to cultivate roses. I could not have chosen a more unfortunate flower. Fashion," he said, "is capricious."

The thought of the capsules reminded me of an anecdote that I had heard. Puss and I had read Veblen together. We had hidden the book under the mattress and read it in the toilet behind locked doors. We had risen early, morning after morning, to watch for the dawn – a dawn exploding over our well-clipped lawn and gashing the hollyhocks with splinters of light. We foreswore our heritage, played commuters, hobnobbed with the gardener and the cook, and damned the family dog as one of the symbols of our class. I thought the story might amuse Puss.

He had taken a capsule out of his pocket and was scratching around in the earth with his nail-file.

"Isn't it disgusting?" I asked, setting his mind in advance. "I have a friend who has a friend who bought aureomycin for her dog. Think of the expense. Think of the children who need milk. The dog died."

"I have," he said turning from his rose bushes, "superannuated social consciousness and sent it to hook mats in the home for senior citizens. I concentrate on growing things. The individual unconscious is in tune with these."

Our mother had opened her window.

"You will take cold," she said.

"To lie in cold obstruction –" said Oedipus.

"And rot," she said leaning over the sill and pointing at Oedipus with her knitting needle. "I read Shakespeare in school before you were born in the days when most girls didn't. I cut the sleeves off my night gown. I smoked with your father after dinner. You only think you are modern. You will catch cold standing around in your shirt sleeves."

Puss's wife called us in for coffee.

"You depend on me," she said to Oedipus, "for everything."

He shrugged his shoulders.

"While you care for the roses and stand about under

the willow," she said, "I must care for both of us. You promised to take out the garbage."

"I have lost interest in ash cans and their contents," said Oedipus. "But the cats which come to the cans are a different matter."

"Do you ever feel," he said, facing his wife, "the cat stirring within you? The individual unconscious," he said, "is peopled with strange shapes."

He turned to me.

"The dog," he said, "I still despise. It has stayed too long among the fairies and has become a god. It lifts its leg against my rose bushes."

He picked up the bag of garbage.

"Has anyone asked you to sit down?" he said.

"You are one of the family," his wife said to me. "You don't have to be asked."

Oedipus went out with the bag.

"I wish," she said, leaning over the coffee cup as she handed it to me, "that your brother Oedipus could be more normal."

"Normal?" I asked.

"Yes," she said, "like you and me."

"He won't even settle to a game of canasta," she said. "He is interested only in the garden and himself. He gives no reason for anything. He only argues. At the moment he is quarrelling with your mother about the willow."

I muttered something about solipsism though I wasn't very sure about the meaning of the word.

She tossed it aside, however.

"Perhaps that's the technical term," she said, "but I think it's selfishness. No one understands what I have to put up with. Your mother certainly doesn't. She evades the subject. I tell you he's dangerous. He will decide nothing. 'Tell your mother the tree is a valuable asset,' I tell him. But he is so wrapped up in himself that he pays no attention."

"You say he depends on you," I reminded her. "This at least is an extroversion. Why don't you tell our mother yourself about the tree."

"Me, me again," she said. "Nothing would be done if I didn't do it. I have to see that the insurance premiums are paid – and even the taxes."

"He would move if he could," I said. "And the individual unconscious scorns insurance. It is insured by the great vegetation myth which promises more than any insurance company can offer."

"You sound like Oedipus," she said. "Perhaps you aren't normal like me, but mad like Oedipus. Your mother is wrong. She thinks it's alcohol. That is merely a symptom – a symptom of a greater disorder. He has never grown up. Like her he refuses to face facts. He looks at the tree as a child would. The tree has an intrinsic value, but he thinks nothing of that."

"Perhaps," I said, "he is looking for a centre."

She glanced up from her coffee cup and reached with the tongs for a lump of sugar. The brown liquid seeped into the angular cube. She looked absently at the dissolving form and stirred the coffee briskly with her spoon.

"But why?" she asked. "He has me – and my friends. Yet what does he do? When I ask people in, when I try to draw a circle around us, what does he do? He argues. He imposes his ideas on everyone. When we discuss pressure cookers or the cost of living, he talks of –"

"The cost of living," Oedipus said as he came through the door, "is an ambiguous phrase. You see it in terms of the price set on steak tenderloin and frozen strawberries, not in the term of the animal and berry itself, not in terms of your own fibre and mine which is endlessly consumed by the very fact that we share our life with the cow and, like the berry, ripen to decay."

"You have been drinking again," she said. "Your bushes are simply an excuse. God knows what you have hidden in the garden."

The doorbell rang. It was our mother.

"I don't like interrupting," she said, "but the plumber says it's the roots of the willow. It has disturbed the whole system. He won't say how much it will cost, but whatever it is, it will be more than I can afford."

"We live on a rented plot," said Oedipus.

"I thought," said our mother, "you owned the house. But no one tells me anything."

"We would not," said Puss's wife, "if I did not pay the taxes. If I didn't work we would live on the mercy of the state."

"The state has no mercy," said Oedipus. "It is a fiction, not a living thing. Only the living have mercy."

"If you must discuss these affairs," said our mother, "discuss them in private. I came about the willow."

"If we pull it up," said Oedipus, "there will be a tunnel between this house and yours."

"You can't pull it up," said our mother. "It must be cut down."

"We were talking," said Oedipus, "when you came in about the cost of living."

"The point under discussion," said our mother, "is the cost of dying. The tree must go and you must pay to have it removed. You must pay, too, for the repair of my drains. This is not a subject I care to dwell upon."

"But we must dwell on it," said Puss's wife. "We must face up to facts – all of us. Are you asking us to sacrifice the tree and to pay for the sacrifice into the bargain?"

"Nothing could be clearer," said our mother.

"The property will decline in value," said Puss's wife. "The tree is an asset – valuable landscaping. It shades the garden and insures privacy. Besides we must get a tree surgeon."

"I said nothing about a tree surgeon," said our mother. "I merely asked to have the tree cut down."

"A surgeon," said Oedipus, "interferes with the natural cycle of growth and decay. He is a thing monstrous in nature and tolerable only because of the perverted philosophy which we inherit from that barbarous age, the age of reason. That age set loose a whole pack of surgeons – the economist, the social reformer, the town planner, the street cleaner, the organizer of departments of public works and the curriculum reformer. Behind it all I see the bland-faced Locke with theories of equal rights and baths for everybody."

"You have been drinking," said our mother.

"He needs an outlet for his emotions," said Puss's wife. "I have asked him to return to the church – *a* church – I don't care which. He can choose which he likes and I will go with him. That's his trouble."

"His trouble is that I spoiled him," said our mother. "He was a bright boy. I was strict as I knew how to be, but was not strict enough – or too strict as the books would tell me now."

"You paid no attention to us at all," said Oedipus. "We grew up as we could."

"You remember only the most unpleasant things," said our mother. "Children have most unfortunate memories. At least, Oedipus, we paid your school bills. Your masters should have taught you something."

"There are three R's," said Oedipus, "which our masters never bothered their heads about – recognition, rejection, and redemption. True, they taught us to look through a microscope, to accept the evidence of our eyes, and to reconcile ourselves to our inferiority."

"A school master would do well," said Puss's wife, "if he taught a boy to brush his teeth and to live within his income."

"My own contemporaries," said Oedipus, "have contributed to the growth of a different idea, though it is perhaps rooted in the same ground. Teachers were to be doctors. They taught nothing, but cured. They were nursemaids with spoons of castor oil. The intolerable neural itch, the exhaustion of weaning were their problems."

"Enough of this," said our mother. "The tree must go. Is my basement to be flooded to satisfy your vanity? We will not refer to the cost."

"We come back again," said Oedipus, "to the word cost. Is living a vanity – or are you referring to my wife's sense of property and your own? Did the tree ask to be planted?"

He went out into the garden. I followed him from the house.

"You know," I said, "Boots, there's some justice in the old lady's complaint."

"Justice?" he asked, looking over his shoulder. "I scorn Plato and his geometrical proportions."

"You are full of scorn," I reminded him.

"Make way," he said with a histrionic gesture waving me forward, "for the Marquis of Carabas."

He knelt down and fumbled among the roses.

"In this I live and breathe," he said, tossing up the earth which was loosely packed around the roots and pulling out a bottle of Vat 69.

"I really hate the old lady," he said, as he screwed the cork out of the bottle, "because of the way she treated our father by bringing us into the world. I keep the willow as a screen. I hope it destroys her whole system so that she moves away from the block."

He corked the bottle, placed it gently among the roots, and tossed the earth back on it.

Our mother was standing on the steps.

"Look in my basement," she said. "That's the place to look."

She came down the steps and walked through the branches of the willow, parting them with her hands.

"Could you turn yourself into a mouse?" asked Oedipus.

She stopped at the gap in the hedge.

"Your wife, Oedipus," she said, "is a fool."

"Turn into a mouse," said Oedipus, "and I will pounce. Then my sensible brother here can inherit the earth and marry the king's daughter, and live happily ever after – and no one will ask him what living happily means."

"I am stranded between the rocks of wife and mother," Oedipus said to me. "If I cut down the tree, my mother will triumph over my wife. She knows her to be as stupid as she is – wise only in the phrase of living – budgets, taxes, ownership. Our mother ignores these things. She has always prided herself on her singularity. We are her children. She is not our mother."

"I can remember," I said, "being attributed to our father when we were difficult. You were right when you said she treated him badly."

"Now," said Puss, "my wife thinks of herself as my father and mother compounded in one clay. She makes herself a graven image before whom I must kneel."

"Have you ever considered," he asked, "the countless dedications: To my wife without whom – *Carissima uxor*. The world is strewed with these votive plaques."

He dug in the earth again and pulled out the Vat 69.

"I suggest," he said, "that the daily papers fall into line with the fashion: To my wife without whose help this eight pound boy –"

He gulped thirstily at the bottle.

"Your wife," I said, "has not helped you to an heir."

"God forbid," he said. "Imagine the household – Big Oedipus and Little Oedipus. One is enough for any generation."

He went to the basement and came out with an axe.

"I will cut down the tree myself," he said. "I will save my mother's system and reduce my wife's taxes."

He laid the axe to the trunk.

Our mother thrust her head out of her window.

"You had better have if done properly," she said. "You will merely take off the foliage and the root will continue to grow."

Puss's wife came to the door.

"I will sell the house first," she said. "Put down that axe."

"Why don't you do something?" they both asked me.

"Why do you stand there?" asked our mother.

"Doing nothing," said Puss's wife.

"The world," shouted Puss, "is a vast amphitheatre. We are all actors in a rite. My sensible brother here is a mere spectator."

Puss's wife shut her door.

"You have been drinking," said our mother. "Bring that axe here."

Oedipus chipped away at the bark. Then he laid down the axe and rooted for his bottle.

"What a scene about nothing," he said. "The individual unconscious scorns such complications."

He sat down by the rose bushes.

The Black Farm

W E MISCALCULATED our Uncle Daedalus. When a man has trafficked in light and colour and softness he may tire of them at last. He may see God, not in the port-hole lights of heaven, but in the black keel which nightly bearing down on him forces him back below the coloured fishes of day's flood, or, deeper still, into the eyeless sockets beneath the sea itself.

I looked for a motive after our uncle had destroyed himself. When he began to build the Black Farm I thought he was playing one of his foolish tricks and that he would succeed somehow; and success, as my brother Oedipus was quick to point out – not without some ambiguity since he had meddled more than anyone suspected in the affair – needs no justification but itself.

You would have to know our Uncle Daedalus to understand. He was, as Oedipus said, sculptured all round and broadloom from ear to ear. He had, Oedipus said, a split-level mind. He wanted the best of both worlds and revenue besides. He talks of vistas, but his windows are shopkeepers' windows built for display,

31

Oedipus said. He buys and sells view lots in a cemetery. He cuts down trees so that his foolish pansies can smile and wink for a day. He can leave nothing as it is.

Our mother made excuses for our uncle.

After all, she said, the turkey carpet on which we took our first steps has worn thin. The marble basin in the bathroom is cracked.

Replacement is a law of life, Puss admitted, but what does our uncle care for that. Replacement for him is a sales' factor – nothing more.

It's curious, our mother said, how often self-made men come on truth through the back door. Daedalus picked up what he knows like agates off a beach. No one bothered about his education. He was the youngest of the boys. What could he do, she said, except to busy himself with things?

He has done his best to make the world a better place to live in, Puss's wife said.

Better than what? Oedipus asked.

Well, better, she said, than it was when I was a girl. He's made the world better for children. I can remember being jabbed with a button-hook when my mother got me into my leggings.

True enough, Puss said. He's tried to persuade the world that he's made it jab-proof and hole-proof and scratch-proof, that it's crush-resistant and head-resistant and stainless; but he ignores lemon juice and the Siamese cat. He forgets the catechism and original sin.

Our mother raised her eyebrows.

Original sin is not a subject for the dinner table, she said. I remember the catechism I learned and probably Daedalus does too, although his education was neglected. Yet before we leave the subject, she said, may I ask if acknowledgement of man's limitations must become a counsel of despair? You have, she said to Oedipus, no sense of proportion. Must a man live naked because he was born naked?

Job had something to say about that, Oedipus answered.

Refrain from quoting him over your cheese, our mother said. He went clothed himself before the days of his misfortune and after too, I think.

She turned to me. When are you going for your holiday? she asked.

Oedipus rolled the stem of his glass between his thumb and middle finger. If a man could only take a luxury cruise to Eden, he said.

Our mother raised her chin a little.

Europa writes, she said to me, that your uncle has been buying up the land around her.

Buying up the hills? I asked. I didn't think he'd follow me beyond the telephone and the hydro.

It is not likely that he will, our mother said. At bottom I think his investment is some scheme to help Europa. He's always been more or less attached to her since he left home as a boy though she tried to spank him once for tying fire-crackers to the cat's tail. He destroyed a good deal from innocent curiosity your father used to say. He lived, your father said, in the nursery of the imagination.

And like Jack climbing the bean-stalk of success he depended on his native wit to defend him from the ogres which people the universe, Oedipus said.

He was as simple as Dick Wittington, our mother said, and as successful.

She put her napkin down beside her plate and rose. Puss's wife followed her into the living room.

When I think of our uncle, Oedipus said, walking the earth as if he'd been cast by nature for some top-echelon role on the stage where Operations Anthropos has gone into the twentieth century of recorded production, I can only wonder that he's not booed from the stage.

I must admit that I hoped by visiting Europa to escape for a bit into Eden myself. I was prepared to find the serpent of course, curled squat about some flowering branch. He's the necessary tension in any Eden. It's the shock of finding him in an aspidistra that can't be borne, or turning him up in a pot of African violets. I wasn't prepared, however, despite my mother's comment, to find my uncle or to be followed by him. I could, if I wanted to, level an inkpot any day at the devil, but before the dove-like simplicity of my uncle I was powerless. I had no recourse against him but retreat.

Europa met me and drove me into the hills. I saw no difference in her. She was simply and magnificently old as a tree is this season and next.

I've come, I said, because I want to get away from it all. I need to let the old Brahma bull in me loose for a little. I can't stand the maze. I'll compound any day for a simple barbed wire fence.

The hills hunched indifferent shoulders about us.

They resent intrusion, Europa said. She pointed to some thistles in a field of hay. Somehow or other, she said, they resist exploitation. They revenge themselves in the end.

I asked her about Daedalus's speculations.

It was one way of saving the hills, she said. I couldn't buy the land myself, so I asked Daedalus to help. His buying the land will protect it from others, she added. It is still in the family. I am sure he'll never want to live here himself; the hills will be free for a generation at least.

When we reached her verandah we turned to look at the sweep of the land. Light burned along the grass and flamed up the thin stems of the poplars. It licked over into the dark coulees and smouldered in the thick mat of wolf willow.

We drank raspberry wine together.

I like to think, Europa said, that I live without the help of Daedalus and his friends but I can't forget poor Thoreau and his axe.

After I had changed my things she helped me saddle.

You won't get far by yourself, she said, but I've a cow to milk and sandwiches to make. Keep to the black path and turn back at the soggy spring. You can't miss either.

I rode off without comment.

Mind the gates, she called after me, and don't bring back a bouquet of deadly camus.

I'll leave that for Daedalus, I answered. He could probably distil it into something innocently sweet as Adam's rib.

I let the horse jog off with me. The thought of my uncle was enough to upset me.

I followed Europa's instructions. And when I got back I unsaddled and turned the horse into the upper pasture. But when I walked into the house there he was – Uncle Daedalus sitting in one of Europa's hand-made chairs and sipping a glass of raspberry wine.

Those who know . . . he was saying. My entrance interrupted him.

How did you get here? I asked.

The question's not how I got here, but why I came, he said. When I heard you were coming I couldn't resist coming too. I keep my ear to the ground, he said.

What a preposterous picture language can evoke, Europa said. You mean you keep your hand on the telephone. But you won't be able to here.

I don't know that I want to, Daedalus answered. Although remember, he added, I'm a born innovator and could change all that if I wanted to. I turned the city into a little country with my planting areas and my barbecues. I could change the hills I suppose. You've no idea, he said, how my planting areas and barbecues took on.

I'm sure, Europa said. Human beings have a curious passion for picnics and potted plants.

Our uncle looked at her approvingly.

You've got the idea, he said. There's no limit to human desire. But human beings don't know what they want. They sleep and dream but they leave it to men like Freud and me to find out what they are really dreaming about. They sleep, he said, and dream; but they sleep on rubber foam now instead of straw.

You'll sleep on a felt mattress here, Europa said, and if your feet are cold at this altitude you warm them on a hot brick. We keep our traditions in the hills.

Are you sure? Daedalus asked. Do you begin to make bread by putting a handful of loose hops in a muslin bag?

Europa ignored his question. I still pick wild strawberries, she said, on my knees among the bluebells and bedstraw. I've crawled on my knees over the better part of a quarter section. Everyone should do it sometime in his life. There are some pleasures, she said, that you can't buy.

Not many, Daedalus said. Besides if you have a passion for picking strawberries you can grow them in a barrel in your own patio. Some of the new varieties are tremendous, he said. In no time at all we'll have single berries as big as a saddle of mutton.

I'm surprised you remember that symbol, Europa said as if she were cutting off the solid white fat and putting it at the side of her plate.

You're in cattle country, I reminded my uncle. Mutton is not esteemed here and lamb even less since it frolics into muttonhood at last. A hogshead of mint sauce wouldn't sweeten the thought.

Europa silenced me with a gesture.

I was thinking, she said, how intractable mutton is in large pieces. I should have thought you would have discarded the idea of saddles and haunches when you and your colleagues advocated a pressure cooker for every stove and a garbage disposal unit for every sink.

You may laugh if you like, Daedalus said. There's not much unpleasantness in the world that can't be chopped and minced and drained away. As a matter of fact no one wants to be bothered with saddles and haunches. I can hardly remember the cuts myself. It's funny, he said, how ideas slip back into a person's mind.

I'm old fashioned, Europa said. I know the power of naphtha soap and ammonia, of borax and banana oil, of peroxide and javell water. I've used Fuller's earth, and sour milk and molasses, but grass stain and blood stain and mildew persist.

Your reagents are mere makeshifts, Daedalus said. It is easy enough to set everything right with a little detergent and some household tools.

So that I could live every day, Europa said, as if I had never lived before.

Daedalus looked at her.

No, he said, so that you could live every day as if you had just begun and everything was ahead of you.

I feel as if everything is ahead of me here, he said. I own all the land now except what still belongs to you.

And I could make an offer for that too that you mightn't like to turn down.

I'm getting tired of gadgets, he said, even the big ones. I've made my money, he said, and now I want to spend it. After all a man's only got a limited time to spend what he has before he dies. I might divide the land up and start a sort of hill city here for people who were tired of the plains.

How could you do that without making money? I asked him.

Where would I go? Europa asked.

Uncle Daedalus sat back in his chair.

I don't suppose you're different from the rest of the world, he said. Most people want a change; most people want a new model after a bit unless they have a taste for antiques and it's not usually the people who have heirlooms who want them. Take the prairies, he said. People there wanted to climb off their tractors into their cars after they'd thrown away their wagon wheels to bring in the tractor. We sold them machinery until they didn't want it anymore; till they got to hate it the way a man hates a nagging wife. We'd saturated the market as the scientist would say. There wasn't much we could give them after we'd given them the combine except a trip to Bermuda or a winter at Palm Springs. So we did and started a reverse reaction. We converted half a ton of tractor seats into household chairs and a carload of wheels into chesterfield frames and we sold them to people who'd only seen wheat ground into flour or steers cut up into roasts and steaks and roped down under cellophane in the groceteria. We've sold the West to thousands of people, he said. I could sell the hills if I wanted.

I couldn't help interrupting him.

As Puss says you've been buying and selling sentiment for years, I told him. You've done a bargain basement business in hearts and flowers. Now you're going to sell men back the simplicity you've cheated them out of just as you sold them back barbaric masks and patterned prayer rugs.

Uncle Daedalus put down his glass.

You forget the time factor, he said. We're selling some things to some people for the first time. If you'd never had freedom there might be something in trying to buy it by the half acre. If you'd always trimmed your nails and listened to dull sermons you might want an African mask or a genuine prayer rug.

In my day it was brummagen brass, Europa said.

Daedalus ignored her.

Oedipus was spoiled, he said. There are people who make up their minds to be satisfied with nothing. In the end a man might as well take them off his mailing list. There are enough people with built-in needs, he said, to make people like Oedipus of no account at all.

Europa picked up the lamp to go for some sandwiches. I didn't wait for them. I went to bed. The next morning I got her to drive me down to the station.

He'll ruin you, I said.

She only laughed. I'm rather fond of Daedalus, she

said. He was an amusing boy. Since he didn't know what others knew he was always drunk with the wonder of the commonplace.

When I got home I called Oedipus on the telephone.

I thought you'd gone beyond the phone and the hydro, he said.

But not beyond the grapevine and the moccasin telegraph, I answered. Nor for that matter beyond the power of automatic transmission. Uncle D. pulled in just behind me.

Trying to look as rustic as a mallard in a cord shirt and slacks no doubt, he said.

He's more like an osprey, I said. The mallard keeps its feet tucked up.

I'd give anything, Oedipus said, to have been squatting in a duck blind when he flew over. I'd have winged him, he said, and I'd do it yet if I could hold the sights firm.

You never would, I said.

And in the end there was no need because Daedalus destroyed himself. I think now with shame of the lightness of our conversation and the narrowness of our apprehension. I would like to forget. I am of slight build with too little steel in my bones to bear the weight of truth. I see now dimly that Oedipus railed at our uncle because he saw in him what I think poets have called his own antimask. He railed. Then he interfered. But to do him justice he was left shaken by the whole affair and his own part in it.

The first news of our uncle's decision came from Europa. I have persuaded Daedalus, Europa wrote, to consolidate his holdings. I have convinced him that subdivision is the symbol of death. He has certain prejudices which I have found it difficult to overcome. If subdivision is the symbol of death he argues, perhaps some must die so that others may have life more abundantly. But it is a demonstrable fact that no one ever found abundance of life in a six foot plot.

For once, Oedipus said laying down the letter which had been addressed to our mother, Daedalus may have lost a victory for a truth he can hardly understand. It is not until the coping closes round us that we begin to live. Could it be that our uncle is developing a sense of values other than those chalked up in the broker's window?

You jump to conclusions, I said to Puss. I don't trust our uncle's prejudice any more than I trust Europa's analogy. The amoeba reproduced by the simple process of division.

Puss groaned.

And you call that life, he said. The daughters of Amoeba shall inherit the earth.

I'm sure, I said, that Uncle Daedalus won't lose it.

I was wrong. He did, but not as one might have thought from incompetence or greed and not at once. He became possessed instead of possessing and all that is left now is the ruin of the Black Farm and the memory of a man who perished in a night he had created for himself.

After Oedipus had read our mother's letter he borrowed his wife's convertible and drove up to see Daedalus, who was still staying with Europa. He said that Europa's talk of death had upset our uncle completely. I was quite right, he said, the old fellow is really beginning to realize that there are eternal verities. But habit is strong. He talks wildly about building some sort of showplace on his property, some monument for posterity – something unusual and striking – the house black, all the fittings black, black flowers in the garden, black hens on the roost, herds of black cattle, black dogs on the lawns, and, in contrast, everything reserved for the master gold so that he may shine like a wrought monogram on a rich velvet ground.

I've told him, Oedipus said, that he's stood behind a stall in the market place too long; he has wasted his money and squandered his ingenuity in the great toy shops of the world. He has spent his life like a magician in various transformations. Now that Europa has persuaded him to consolidate his holdings into an estate I have advised him to devote his skill and his money to the discovery of values and the pursuit of truth. This is the very thing I would do myself, Oedipus said, if I had the time and the money.

I found it difficult to think of our uncle with an estate of any kind. Whatever his ancestors have been, he could certainly have no real conception of himself as a country squire or even as a gentleman farmer. If he succeeded in carrying out the idea of the Black Farm he would be nothing but a Sancho Panza with a kingdom of blackamoors. I found it ludicrous to think of him, too, as searching for truth with his assembly-line tools and weighing what he found in the grocers' scales of his past experience. However, Oedipus's visit seemed to set him in motion. Up to that time he had moved about his affairs sometimes by oscillation, sometimes by rotary synthesis. Now he assumed direction. And his imagination, set going by Oedipus, carried him by a sort of jet propulsion into a darkness as black as Pluto's acres.

The difficulty, he said to me when he met me in town one day, is to find true black. I used to live by a decorator's chart. What the experts said was good enough. Since I've started my project, I see quite plainly that you can't change a blonde into a brunette by dyeing her hair. Colour, he said, can't be rubbed on. It's the thing itself. It's curious, he said, where real thought takes one.

He looked for horses, dogs, and hens – all of uniform blackness – without much success. He had no trouble in finding gold. He bought himself a palomino. The sun only altered the quality of its fire, which in winter glowed with a little more warmth, in summer with a softer brightness. Brief as a horse's life is, though, he was not himself to live long enough to test the real quality of the gold. For the time being he had no quarrel with it. But his black horses faded and the slightest gall patched them with white.

He explored blackness in all its manifestations. I don't know where he came by his information. Probably he read in the public library for our mother saw him there one day surrounded by encyclopaedias and guides to science and the arts which I think he had never turned over before except for information incidental to his business. He had as we knew a wealth of knowledge about Roman brick and Botticelli caps and other trivia connected with his ventures.

Now he was becoming global in his research. He began to import materials for the farm. Since he could find no suitable wood for his house he sent to the Black Pasture quarries in Northumberland for marble. When the marble had been raised on its foundations he found that the surface reflected the green of the trees and the crimson of the evening sky. He cut down the trees but the sky was beyond reach of his workmen. He imported blackcocks from Asia only to find that they had white wing patches and vermilion eyebrows. He hired boys to trap blackbirds for him but the birds' beaks were gamboge yellow and the females various shades of brown. He sent to India for black buck but the young males when they were unloaded from the plane were yellowish fawn and would, he found on further inquiry, deepen into black only with age. He collected black nightshade, which poisoned him with its leaves and blossomed into flowers as white as innocence.

I have set myself to find a natural uniformity, he said, against which my person might shine with the glory of heaven. Nature resists me at every turn.

Europa told us that he had imported servants from Haiti and the heart of dark Africa, but that the whites of their eyes were a continual distraction to him. The Labrador dogs, too, which lay about his door, stared at him out of amber eyes. She thought, she said, that the whole enterprise had been a whim and harmless – an innocent fancy which would keep him busy and save the hills from exploitation for a while at least.

He had stopped going to the library and remained, as far as any of us knew, in the marble house which continued to reflect the sky. He was, the report came, under the tutelage of one of his white-eyed servants making excursions into black magic. If nature would not co-operate with him he would find ways of exacting submission from her.

He had ordered a number of black earthenware pots. Europa had seen the bill of lading at the station when she drove in to pick up a saddle she herself had ordered. And while she was still in the station one of the servants had ridden in on Daedalus's palomino to pick up the *govi* as he called them for his master. She herself had taken them in the car despite the man's protests, fearing, as she said, that he would break them. It had given her a start, she said, to see the black man on a palomino like a devil riding the sun.

Daedalus, she felt, had not been pleased to see her when she drove in with the pots; but she had stayed long enough, she said, to drink a very bad cup of tea which one of the servants finally brought. She had asked him what he intended to do with the pots and he had remarked succinctly that he was going to have a family reunion. She reported that he looked thin and pale and generally out of sorts. She had asked him why his man had referred to the pots as *govi*. He had hedged a little and then become voluble, almost incoherent, in his speech.

A single one of the pots, he assured her, had more value than a university education – certainly more value than anyone would set on the scraps of information he had managed to pick up in his various projects. The whole family, he said, had scorned him because, although he had been successful in practical affairs – more successful than any of them – he had no sense of value. These men of mine, he said, can summon into these pots all our ancestral *loa* – the active spirits of our race. Once I have them in these pots behind locked doors I can extract from them in a moment more knowledge of eternal verities than Oedipus ever dreamed up under his rose bushes. Ghede has already chosen me, he said, the eternal figure in black.

Who, wrote Europa, is Ghede? I am afraid that Daedalus's financial worries and his isolation are having a serious effect on his constitution. I thought, she wrote, that he was simply playing with magic as a child plays with a tinker-toy or the chemistry sets which are sold at Christmas in most department stores.

Who, echoed our mother, is Ghede?

He is, said Oedipus, death at the cross roads. He stands at the intersection of time and eternity. He is corpse and phallus, king and clown. He introduces men to their own devil. He is the last day of the week and the cross in every cemetery. He sings the song of the grave digger.

Next Europa reported that drums were beating incessantly in the hills. Her amused tolerance had become concern. She had ridden over to see Daedalus but the black servants had refused to let her pass through the black marble vestibule into the house itself. The master, they said, had left orders not to be disturbed. She had seen the palomino cropping grass in the pasture, but had noted nothing else except the frightful mess made by the felled trees which had sheltered the house, and a black rooster fattening in a pen where Daedalus had intended to build a marble patio. All was quiet; but as she rode through the gate into what had once been her old lease she heard the drums chuckling behind her.

With her letter came one from Daedalus himself addressed to Oedipus. It was written in white ink on what seemed to be the folded page of a cheap photograph album. The message was brief:

> *The god of the abyss has spoken. All black is white.*
> *There are no eternal verities.*

Oedipus stood holding the paper.

He has cried out to the god, Oedipus said, but the echo of his own voice has drowned the answer. I must drive down and put an end to this business.

But that very night Daedalus set fire to the long grass in his pasture.

Antigone

MY FATHER RULED a kingdom on the right bank of the river. He ruled it with a firm hand and a stout heart though he was often more troubled than Moses, who was simply trying to bring a stubborn and moody people under God's yoke. My father ruled men who thought they were gods or the instruments of gods or, at very least, god-afflicted and god-pursued. He ruled Atlas who held up the sky, and Hermes who went on endless messages, and Helen who'd been hatched from an egg, and Pan the gardener, and Kallisto the bear, and too many others to mention by name. Yet my father had no thunderbolt, no trident, no helmet of darkness. His subjects were delivered bound into his hands. He merely watched over them as the hundred-handed ones watched over the dethroned Titans so that they wouldn't bother Hellas again.

Despite the care which my father took to maintain an atmosphere of sober common sense in his whole establishment, there were occasional outbursts of self-indulgence which he could not control. For instance,

I have seen Helen walking naked down the narrow cement path under the chestnut trees for no better reason, I suppose, than that the day was hot and the white flowers themselves lay naked and expectant in the sunlight. And I have seen Atlas forget the sky while he sat eating the dirt which held him up. These were things which I was not supposed to see.

If my father had been as sensible through and through as he was thought to be, he would have packed me off to boarding school when I was old enough to be disciplined by men. Instead he kept me at home with my two cousins who, except for the accident of birth, might as well have been my sisters. Today I imagine people concerned with our welfare would take such an environment into account. At the time I speak of most people thought us fortunate – especially the girls whose fathers' affairs had come to an unhappy issue. I don't like to revive old scandal and I wouldn't except to deny it; but it takes only a few impertinent newcomers in any community to force open cupboards which had been decently sealed by time. However, my father was so busy setting his kingdom to rights that he let weeds grow up in his own garden.

As I said, if my father had had all his wits about him he would have sent me to boarding school – and Antigone and Ismene too. I might have fallen in love with the headmaster's daughter and Antigone might have learned that no human being can be right always. She might have found out besides that from the seeds of eternal justice grow madder flowers than any which Pan grew in the gardens of my father's kingdom.

Between the kingdom which my father ruled and the wilderness flows a river. It is this river which I am crossing now. Antigone is with me.

How often can we cross the same river, Antigone asks.

Her persistence annoys me. Besides, Heraklitos made nonsense of her question years ago. He saw a river too – the Inachos, the Kephissos, the Lethaios. The name doesn't matter. He said: See how quickly the water flows. However agile a man is, however nimbly he swims, or runs, or flies, the water slips away before him. See, even as he sets down his foot the water is displaced by the stream which crowds along in the shadow of its flight.

But after all, Antigone says, one must admit that it is the same kind of water. The oolichan run in it as they ran last year and the year before. The gulls cry above the same banks. Boats drift towards the Delta and circle back against the current to gather up the catch.

At any rate, I tell her, we're standing on a new bridge. We are standing so high that the smell of mud and river weeds passes under us out to the straits. The unbroken curve of the bridge protects the eye from details of river life. The bridge is foolproof as a clinic's passport to happiness.

The old bridge still spans the river, but the cat-walk with its cracks and knot-holes, with its gap between planking and hand-rail has been torn down. The centre arch still grinds open to let boats up and down the river, but a child can no longer be walked on it or swung out on it beyond the water-gauge at the very centre of the flood.

I've known men who scorned any kind of bridge, Antigone says. Men have walked into the water, she says, or, impatient, have jumped from the bridge into the river below.

But these, I say, didn't really want to cross the river. They went Persephone's way, cradled in the current's arms, down the long halls under the pink feet of the gulls, under the booms and tow-lines, under the soft bellies of the fish.

Antigone looks at me.

There's no coming back, she says, if one goes far enough.

I know she's going to speak of her own misery and I won't listen. Only a god has the right to say: Look what I suffer. Only a god should say: What more ought I to have done for you that I have not done?

Once in winter, she says, a man walked over the river.

Taking advantage of nature, I remind her, since the river had never frozen before.

Yet he escaped from the penitentiary, she says. He escaped from the guards walking round the walls or standing with their guns in the sentry-boxes at the four corners of the enclosure. He escaped.

Not without risk, I say. He had to test the strength of the ice himself. Yet safer perhaps than if he had crossed by the old bridge where he might have slipped through a knot-hole or tumbled out through the railing.

He did escape, she persists, and lived forever on the far side of the river in the Alaska tea and bulrushes. For where, she asks, can a man go farther than to the outermost edge of the world?

The habitable world, as I've said, is on the right bank of the river. Here is the market with its market stalls – the coops of hens, the long-tongued geese, the haltered calf, the bearded goat, the shoving pigs, and the empty bodies of cows and sheep and rabbits hanging on iron hooks. My father's kingdom provides asylum in the suburbs. Near it are the convent, the churches, and the penitentiary. Above these on the hill the cemetery looks down and on the river itself.

It is a world spread flat, tipped up into the sky so that men and women bend forward, walking as men walk when they board a ship at high tide. This is the world I feel with my feet. It is the world I see with my eyes.

I remember standing once with Antigone and Ismene in the square just outside the gates of my father's kingdom. Here from a bust set high on a cairn the stone eyes of Simon Fraser look from his stone face over the river that he found.

It is the head that counts, Ismene said.

It's no better than an urn, Antigone said, one of the urns we see when we climb to the cemetery above.

And all I could think was that I didn't want an urn, only a flat green grave with a chain about it.

A chain won't keep out the dogs, Antigone said.

But his soul could swing on it, Ismene said, like a bird blown on a branch in the wind.

And I remember Antigone's saying: The cat drags its belly on the ground and the rat sharpens its tooth in the ivy.

I should have loved Ismene, but I didn't. It was Antigone I loved. I should have loved Ismene because, although she walked the flat world with us, she managed somehow to see it round.

The earth is an oblate spheroid, she'd say. And I knew that she saw it there before her comprehensible and whole like a tangerine spiked through and held in place while it rotated on the axis of one of Nurse's steel sock needles. The earth was a tangerine and she saw the skin peeled off and the world parcelled out into neat segments, each segment sweet and fragrant in its own skin.

It's the head that counts, she said.

In her own head she made diagrams to live by, cut and fashioned after the eternal patterns spied out by Plato as he rummaged about in the sewing basket of the gods.

I should have loved Ismene. She would live now in some prefabricated and perfect chrysolite by some paradigm which made love round and whole. She would simply live and leave destruction in the purgatorial ditches outside her own walled paradise.

Antigone is different. She sees the world flat as I do and feels it tip beneath her feet. She has walked in the market and seen the living animals penned and the dead hanging stiff on their hooks. Yet she defies what she sees with a defiance which is almost denial. Like Atlas she tries to keep the vaulted sky from crushing the flat earth. Like Hermes she brings a message that there is life if one can escape to it in the brush and bulrushes in some dim Hades beyond the river. It is defiance not belief and I tell her that this time we walk the bridge to a walled cave where we can deny death no longer.

Yet she asks her questions still. And standing there I tell her that Heraklitos has made nonsense of her question. I should have loved Ismene for she would have taught me what Plato meant when he said in all earnest that the union of the soul with the body is in no way better than dissolution. I expect that she understood things which Antigone is too proud to see.

I turn away from her and flatten my elbows on the high wall of the bridge. I look back at my father's kingdom. I see the terraces rolling down from the red-brick buildings with their barred windows. I remember hands shaking the bars and hear fingers tearing up paper and stuffing it through the meshes. Diktynna, mother of nets and high leaping fear. O Artemis, mistress of wild beasts and wild men.

The inmates are beginning to come out on the screened verandahs. They pace up and down in straight lines or stand silent like figures which appear at the same time each day from some depths inside a clock.

On the upper terrace Pan the gardener is shifting sprinklers with a hooked stick. His face is shadowed by the brim of his hat. He moves as economically as an animal between the beds of lobelia and geranium. It is high noon.

Antigone has cut out a piece of sod and has scooped out a grave. The body lies in a coffin in the shade of the magnolia tree. Antigone and I are standing. Ismene is sitting between two low angled branches of the monkey puzzle tree. Her lap is filled with daisies. She slits the stem of one daisy and pulls the stem of another through it. She is making a chain for her neck and a crown for her hair.

Antigone reaches for a branch of the magnolia. It is almost beyond her grip. The buds flame above her. She stands on a small fire of daisies which smoulder in the roots of grass.

I see the magnolia buds. They brood above me, whiteness feathered on whiteness. I see Antigone's face turned to the light. I hear the living birds call to the sun. I speak private poetry to myself: Between four trumpeting angels at the four corners of the earth a bride stands before the altar in a gown as white as snow.

Yet I must have been speaking aloud because Antigone challenges me: You're mistaken. It's the winds the angels hold, the four winds of the earth. After the just are taken to paradise the winds will destroy the earth. It's a funeral, she says, not a wedding.

She looks towards the building.

Someone is coming down the path from the matron's house, she says.

I notice that she has pulled one of the magnolia blossoms from the branch. I take it from her. It is streaked with brown where her hands have bruised it. The sparrow which she has decided to bury lies on its back. Its feet are clenched tight against the feathers of its breast. I put the flower in the box with it.

Someone is coming down the path. She is wearing a blue cotton dress. Her cropped head is bent. She walks slowing carrying something in a napkin.

It's Kallisto the bear, I say. Let's hurry. What will my father say if he sees us talking to one of his patients?

If we live here with him, Antigone says, what can he expect? If he spends his life trying to tame people he can't complain if you behave as if they were tame. What would your father think, she says, if he saw us digging in the Institution lawn?

Pan comes closer. I glower at him. There's no use speaking to him. He's deaf and dumb.

Listen, I say to Antigone, my father's not unreasonable. Kallisto thinks she's a bear and he thinks he's a bear tamer, that's all. As for the lawn, I say quoting my father without conviction, a man must have order among his own if he is to keep order in the state.

Kallisto has come up to us. She is smiling and laughing to herself. She gives me her bundle.

Fish, she says.

I open the napkin.

Pink fish sandwiches, I say.

For the party, she says.

But it isn't a party, Antigone says. It's a funeral.

For the funeral breakfast, I say.

Ismene is twisting two chains of daisies into a rope. Pan has stopped pulling the sprinkler about. He is standing beside Ismene resting himself on his hooked stick. Kallisto squats down beside her. Ismene turns away, preoccupied, but she can't turn far because of Pan's legs.

> *Father said we never should*
> *Play with madmen in the wood.*

I look at Antigone.

It's my funeral, she says.

I go over to Ismene and gather up a handful of loose daisies from her lap. The sun reaches through the shadow of the magnolia tree.

It's my funeral, Antigone says. She moves possessively towards the body.

An ant is crawling into the bundle of sandwiches which I've put on the ground. A file of ants is marching on the sparrow's box.

I go over and drop daisies on the bird's stiff body. My voice speaks ritual words: Deliver me, O Lord, from everlasting death on this dreadful day. I tremble and am afraid.

The voice of a people comforts me. I look at Antigone. I look her in the eye.

It had better be a proper funeral then, I say.

Kallisto is crouched forward on her hands. Tears are running down her cheeks and she is licking them away with her tongue.

My voice rises again: I said in the midst of my days, I shall not see —

Antigone just stands there. She looks frightened, but her eyes defy me with their assertion.

It's my funeral, she says. It's my bird. I was the one who wanted to bury it.

She is looking for a reason. She will say something which sounds eternally right.

Things have to be buried, she says. They can't be left lying around anyhow for people to see.

Birds shouldn't die, I tell her. They have wings. Cats and rats haven't wings.

Stop crying, she says to Kallisto. It's only a bird.

It has a bride's flower in its hand, Kallisto says.

We shall rise again, I mutter, but we shall not all be changed.

Antigone does not seem to hear me.

Behold, I say in a voice she must hear, in a moment, in the twinkling of an eye, the trumpet shall sound.

Ismene turns to Kallisto and throws the daisy chain about her neck.

Shall a virgin forget her adorning or a bride the ornament of her breast?

Kallisto is lifting her arms towards the tree.

The bridegroom has come, she says, white as a fall of snow. He stands above me in a great ring of fire.

Antigone looks at me now.

Let's cover the bird up, she says. Your father will punish us all for making a disturbance.

He has on his garment, Kallisto says, and on his thigh is written King of Kings.

I look at the tree. If I could see with Kallisto's eyes I wouldn't be afraid of death, or punishment, or the penitentiary guards. I wouldn't be afraid of my father's belt or his honing strap or his bedroom slipper. I wouldn't be afraid of falling into the river through a knot-hole in the bridge.

But, as I look, I see the buds falling like burning lamps and I hear the sparrow twittering in its box: Woe, woe, woe because of the three trumpets which are yet to sound.

Kallisto is on her knees. She is growling like a bear. She lumbers over to the sandwiches and mauls them with her paw.

Ismene stands alone for Pan the gardener has gone.

Antigone is fitting a turf in place above the coffin. I go over and press the edge of the turf with my feet. Ismene has caught me by the hand.

Go away, Antigone says.

I see my father coming down the path. He has an attendant with him. In front of them walks Pan holding the sprinkler hook like a spear.

What are you doing here? my father asks.

Burying a bird, Antigone says.

Here? my father asks again.

Where else could I bury it? Antigone says.

My father looks at her.

This ground is public property, he says. No single person has any right to an inch of it.

I've taken six inches, Antigone says. Will you dig the bird up again?

Some of his subjects my father restrained since they were moved to throw themselves from high places or to tear one another to bits from jealousy or rage. Others who disturbed the public peace he taught to walk in the airing courts or to work in the kitchen or in the garden.

If men live at all, my father said, it is because discipline saves their life for them.

From Antigone he simply turned away.

The Rumble Seat

OEDIPUS FOLDED his legs. It was a sad story. He had adjusted himself as the cameras circled. We could not see them but we knew they were there. Information is no longer the prerogative of the few. Besides Oedipus was pointing above him now to something which was excluded from our television screen.

They're like vultures, he said to Pierre. They're like the nuns perched in their choir loft looking down at the squatters in their padded pew.

Pierre's deceptively small image dilated.

Sarcorhampus papa, he prayed to a hidden but hovering shape. Coragyps atratus. Neophron perconopterus. King vulture, black vulture, Egyptian vulture. The litany from *Webster's New Collegiate* rolled sweetly off his tongue.

The sphincter round his mouth tightened.

A-ha, now he's pursing his lips, our uncle mocked.

Oiseau rapace d'Europe et d'Asie. Lâche, prudent, très vorace vautour, Pierre prayed trilling his r's with conviction as he shifted to *Larousse*.

His hand reached for his tie. He looked straight at Oedipus. He was, we observed, despite his deference to the hidden cameras, completely himself.

All the while, Oedipus said, the organ was shaking the church. The foundations were quite unsound.

He stopped as if he had turned back to the story too quickly.

Pappa, pappe, pappepipappe, he murmured. Father, grandfather, great grandfather. He seemed to think that for Pierre's sake he should suggest that it had happened in another country and that perhaps –

Dieu est mort, he added courteously.

Kaput, our uncle translated officiously. And no one has the nerve to pull the plug.

Pierre lifted an ambiguous finger.

Oedipus stared at the small folds of skin between the proximal and middle phalanges. Then his eye moved to the distal end of the ungular phalanx.

We strained closer. The iconoclastic digit was about to strike.

Nail him, our uncle cried. We're being taxed to pump blood through a dead organism. The EEG has been flat as a flounder since Darwin sailed home on the *Beagle*. Oh for the cold end of a hot line. Now's the time.

But Pierre let his hand fall on the circular table.

Panta rei, he said. Everything flows. But not fast enough. Nel mezzo del camin, on the throughway, we still find the Volkswagen with Laius behind the wheel. It is better to be the instrument of fate than its victim.

Oedipus's voice had become a mere rumble. Then it rose suddenly as if some mechanism had adjusted efficiently.

> *He looked at his watch and his watch was slow*
> *He looked at the water and the water was low*
> *Turned to his fireboy –*

With a gesture Pierre interrupted his guest.

Where? he asked turning full into the screen and intoning the stops on the long journey. Vancouver, Westminster, Hope, Yale, North Bend, Lytton, Spence's Bridge, Ashcroft, Kamloops. At length he reached Jackfish, the coldest point on the run.

With total irrelevance Oedipus returned to the initial question:

Reno, he said. It's on another line.

Bien sûr! Ah oui alors! Ne m'en parlez pas. Yes. Yes. Yes.

Beneath its pale circlet of hair Pierre's face was the face of simple faith betrayed. It had the human look. His voice was scrupulous against offence.

Réflexes verbaux de la conversation française, our uncle remarked categorically from his place in front of the set. Provocation and instant retort. The confessionals are empty but the listening posts are crowded. Allons, du calme! Cela passera. Play it cool. Mufle! Abruti! Espèce de menteur! No need to translate. C'est vous qui nous avez trahis! You lied. Jamais. I too was deceived. Un livre de pain par jour ne me suffit pas! I can't live on that. Qu'est-ce qu'il vous fait? The walkout's out. Invade. Il gronde son père maintenant. The father-figure is an anachronism. Il n'y a plus d'enfants. We must open the freezers. La vie nous réserve bien des désillusions. The packaging obscures the content. I was deceived by spinsters. Ce n'est que justice! That's the way the belly buttons.

Pierre's voice reached us through the chatter.

In this country, Pierre said, mass arrogance, bribery, false witness, and perjury are our natural climate. We have no recourse except to a committee of the senate or to an equally outmoded legal code. But you have derailed me. I hesitate to bring up the matter of sex.

Among the solitary bees, Oedipus interrupted, scolies, masons, bembex, anthropores, the males do not hesitate. They range about the nests waiting for the birth of females. When these appear they seize and mount them. Thus the nymphs know life and love in the same shiver.

The image before us began to drift.

Bees, Pierre said, bees. The old nineteenth century approach.

The faces came into focus. The line of Pierre's mouth had settled into a despondent scepticism.

The Catholic Women's League of Canada, he began. The Knights of Columbus. The Anglican Women's Auxiliary of Qu'Appelle and the Diocesan Synods of Huron and Algoma to be fearlessly particular. The ecclesiastical establishment from the centre to the circumference of its pedestrian certitude, unaware of the origins and significance of the sexual revolution, insensitive to ubiquitous erotic stimuli, blind to the taboo-activity already permitted by fraternity-pin relationships, deaf to the voice of sexual starvation, untouched by the anguish of induced or illusory guilt, convinced, despite undisputed genetic truth, that an acquired characteristic, called original sin by that pseudo-modernist T.E. Hulme, if I'm not mistaken –

His voice swept with violence beyond predication.

Oedipus himself turned full into the screen.

Dwellers in our native Thebes, he said, I am Oedipus who knew the famed riddle.

He seemed to be trying out a role.

This is Toronto, Pierre said. Riddles are beside the point. Here we have obstruction, obscurantism, and worse.

We must, he said turning to Oedipus, demythologize.

For me it is too late, Oedipus answered, although since Protestantism has not yet fully acknowledged Freud there might still be time. For some I have already become a complex, for others a thematic design like the sphere, the cylinder, and the cube.

Our uncle hitched his chair closer. The point, the line and the square, he growled in response, looking fixedly at Pierre. Then he turned to us. Pancake make-up and a soft-boiled shirt, he muttered. He was in a rude and irritable mood we could see. His mind would be buzzing all night as he tried to free his antennae from the gluey surface which solicited his attention.

Pierre was regarding Oedipus with an air of bonhomie – indeed with a look of credulous simplicity.

After his unprovoked outburst our uncle had turned back hungrily to the set, his neck shoved forward, his hand lifted.

As you know, Oedipus said to Pierre, I was born and raised inside the walls of a madhouse where the corridors were long and locked before and behind. Can you imagine, he asked, the institutional passage-ways? Can you smell the fume of wax and carbolic? Can you see the wooden panelling and the fat brass doorknobs? Can you endure the light from the naked bulbs on their hanging cords? Can you hear the squeak-ing of rats, the mewing of cats, the howling of dogs? Can you catch the medicinal whiff exhaled from the dispensary below?

Pierre drew his haunches under him like a man whose horse has begun to bolt.

I was brought up, he said, in a little town. Behind the town was a mysterious bear-infested wood. I remember a missionary lady who told me that my dog wouldn't go to heaven because it had no soul. I remember, like Edmund Gosse, losing my faith in prayer. I remember under the guidance of an innovating clergyman joining a Wolf Cub pack and hiking cheerfully to wiener roasts where I once babbled incoherently to a white-bearded God to save me from bears.

Spare us the next episode, cried our uncle. Spare us adolescence, the horse chestnuts, the rubber bands, the chilling experience of sunday-school in Victoria British Columbia. Grammatically speaking we are all past participles. We are adult. Let us get on with the dilemmas and perils, the anguishing and sorrowful problems per omnia saecula saeculorum as Immanuel Kant said.

He threw himself back in his chair. His clamour had prevented us from hearing Oedipus's comment. In fact he had thoroughly distracted us. As he now sat, his head flung against the uncompromising verticals behind him, he seemed to have exhausted his strength. With a spastic jerk, however, he pointed the index of his right hand to Oedipus as if to suggest in both languages: He too is to blame – voilà le coupable.

Go on with your story, Pierre was saying. Our time is limited.

Must we, roared our uncle slanting forward, live by the clock after the clock-maker has been sacked? Are we a mechanical sequence, an organized seriality? Has not Bergson proved beyond a doubt that we are snaky and submarine? The soul of man Berdyaev observed no longer rests on secure foundations. We float, we flood, we flounder. Finally we are redundant.

Our uncle himself had arrived at the perils and anguish. He clasped his hands. Are we, he mourned, flotsam or jetsam? Have we survived or are we being thrown overboard?

His voice rose on a hectoring note. According to modern theory he should have been cool. He was behaving in an unaccountable way.

Are we, he asked, really continuous and fluid? Or are we rigid spatial hollows, skins of the void? Are we structural cages or free standing plinths? Now that you've cracked our shell, stripped off our shingles, peered through our plastic curtains, peeled back the skin from our skulls what do you see?

Between the explosions of our uncle's voice we caught phrases of Oedipus's story: two children passing a reception desk – a flight of stairs – the turning of locks. It was almost impossible to hear.

In the silence which followed our uncle's noisy involvement a bodiless voice asserted itself. The camera was focused on Pierre reacting. We saw him inclining towards the abstracted body, his lips protruding a little, his eyelids pressed up against the inclining slope of his domed and furrowed brow.

There we were, Oedipus's voice was saying, the first time we met God, kneeling on a slippery dance floor, locked in with madmen and madwomen too.

We could see both men now.

It must have been the third sunday after Pentecost, or perhaps the second, I'm not sure, Oedipus went on. The tulips in the garden had been taken up. The daisies, which someone told me first grew in the Pyrenees, were tall enough to hide in. But it must have been the third sunday because when I remember the day I remember the story of the lost sheep.

Pierre interrupted him. I remember that parable too,

he said. The church has taught people to live with their misery. If the church is to survive, he added pontifically, it must cease to comfort and make those it serves acutely uncomfortable.

As I remember it, Oedipus said, the floor on which we knelt was extremely uncomfortable. To begin with it was dusted with boracic acid. The restless flock –

Oedipus, Oedipus, you remind me of the sampling of 248 Anglican ministers I have already questioned. We have our mental health clinics, our brotherhood weeks, our alcoholics anonymous conventions, our community chests and united appeal drives. The camera had brought Pierre's face into full focus. It panned to include Oedipus.

The dancing on saturday was therapeutic I suppose, Oedipus admitted. Like hot baths it was a substitute for the strait jacket and the padded box, or so I learned later. On sunday the priest came to celebrate so we were told. The words therapeutic and celebrate have many curious flowers locked in their roots.

Including the servomotor, our uncle cried.

When we were older, Oedipus continued, we were sent to the parish church on sundays.

We need a new kind of church, Pierre interrupted. The word parish seemed to have upset him. His voice assumed a professorial tone. "A religion," says Yinger in *Religion, Society and the Individual*, "will not hold the allegiance of a group of people who have acquired as the result of non-religious causes, new aesthetic tastes, new intellectual perspectives, new occupational interests, new moral conceptions – unless religion adjusts to those changes." I quote from my own recent study.

Our uncle had begun to show signs of agitation. All the while he had been simmering below the surface like water on the boil.

If the church sanctions social revolution it is only because it seeks protective covering. What you see there is an image of yourself. Trotsky said this or something like it after the revolution. About him he saw God being recreated as a doctor of female ailments, an all-powerful scandal-monger, as a moonlighting administrator. "Here is the apocalypse," quote, "Voltaire, and Darwin and the psalm-book" unquote.

He buried his head in his hands as if to shield himself from his own contradictions.

Quite so, Oedipus said. Our father was much too busy on his wards and in his laboratory to take us to the parish church. Our Presbyterian nurse had objected so strongly to the images as she called them that she had been excused from any obligation to accompany us. She merely hooked us into our leggings and buttoned us into our coats. On sunday morning we were freer than usual. We were the sole occupants of the small hard pew which our father had rented at the middle left of the dilapidated structure. Right next to it, but separated from it by a wooden panel, was an upholstered pew, the Murphys' pew. As we uttered the uncompromising name we always shuddered. The oldest of the Murphy boys was called Spud. He didn't seem to care at all. Perhaps he had been corrupted by his environment.

There was no doubt, Oedipus went on, that the pew looked comfortable. We lusted after it. We charted the Murphys' comings and goings. We had decided to occupy it. The Murphys were devout communicants. They usually went to an early mass. If we can get there at eleven, I told my sister, it's all ours. Besides it will be a high mass and everyone will be listening to the organ. We will be able to reach the pew, unnoticed, by the central aisle.

On Septuagesima sunday which fell that year in late January or early February, it was raining when we woke. Our nurse gave us our oatmeal and waited for the rain to stop. I looked at the clock. It was well after nine. The Murphys would soon be out of their padded pew. Our nurse despite her scruples had hooked us into our leggings and buttoned us into our reefer coats. After a look at the downpour she put my sister's hat back in the closet and fastened her into a raincape with an attached hood. She bundled me into a slicker and sou'wester, unbuttoned my leggings and held my gumboots while I put my feet into them.

It was a long walk to the church. We loitered to watch the water swirl down the drains. When we got to the church the priest was at the altar and the organ was playing in a profound and shattering way. No one could see and stop us now because all the backs were turned to the door. We had walked only a few steps down the centre aisle, however, when the priest turned around. His arms were extended as if in welcome. It was an unexpected courtesy.

The kneeling bench was not quite as soft as I had imagined but the view from the pew down the centre aisle was unobstructed. In a short time everyone sat down. The upholstered seat was soft and warm. A soothing heat flowed over us from a large grated square on which the pew unexpectedly abutted.

The priest who had climbed up the stairs to the pulpit began to talk about the fall of Adam and the sins of the whole human race.

Our uncle had been growing restless. We are adults, he cried, adults. Why do you let him go on. Ask him if he thinks sex is sinful, he demanded. Ask him if he regards the fall of Adam as a literal happening. Question the reaction of his mature intelligence to the fables he was exposed to in his innocence.

The cushioned seat, Oedipus went on, was comforting. The wave of heat from somewhere under the floor, however, was becoming oppressive. My sister had taken off her raincape and her coat and sitting there in her short sleeved white frock was struggling with the buttons of her leggings. I took off my slicker. The heat I noticed seemed to be subsiding. I felt completely happy.

The priest had gone from the sad story of Adam to the story of Noah's flood. I had no doubt that Noah, despite his trials and his excessive age, must have felt safe in the ark surrounded by his family and his creatures. I wondered if the ark was upholstered inside with green baize like the Murphys' pew or with red serge like the dining room curtains. Perhaps it was lined with purple like the priest's vestments so that the coat of the lion, the fleece of the lamb, the hair of the wolf might appear to advantage in the rather close quarters. When I looked at my sister she had stopped trying to take off her leggings and had gone to sleep like one of the fowl or the cattle or the creeping things that Noah had taken into the ark. After the priest had gone and the people were hastening out I had some trouble waking her and helping her into her coat. I picked up my slicker and her cape. I was sure that it had stopped raining and that we wouldn't need them. Never during all the time we had thought of occupying the pew had we ever thought of leaving it. It was then that we saw the two nuns waiting in the doorway. They had seen us from the loft.

They didn't blame us for sitting in the Murphys' pew, Oedipus said. They didn't blame us for being comfortable there. They accused my sister of taking off her coat so that all the poor little girls could see her dress. One nun began unbuttoning and rebuttoning her coat. Just feel the nap, she said. All over the world, she said, children are freezing to death. Aren't you ashamed, she said.

I wanted to say that we had no choice in the matter of our clothing. Fate had given us these skins. Indeed we disliked them more than she ever could. I know now that it was not fate but the long hand of Leeds and

Manchester, extended across half the world into the buttonhook, which pinched us into our leggings just as it stuffed the Tahitian royal family into black wool suits and vests and jammed bowler hats down over their eyes – the same hand that is poking them even now into mini skirts and pantyhose. How could one coat and one dress I wanted to say keep all the children warm.

Pierre was shifting uneasily. He had lost control. In a moment he would have to end the interview. He would have to make some significant gesture before tired, drained, and quiet, as the public press assured us, he would decompress under a spot-light in some darkly elegant bar.

And the Four Animals

THE FOOTHILLS slept. Over their yellow limbs the blue sky crouched. Only a fugitive green suggested life which claimed kinship with both and acknowledged kinship with neither.

Around the curve of the hill, or out of the hill itself, came three black dogs. The watching eye could not record with precision anything but the fact of their presence. Against the faded contour of the earth the things were. The watcher could not have said whether they had come or whether the eye had focused them into being. In the place of the hills before and after have no more meaning than the land gives. Now there were the dogs where before were only the hills and the transparent stir of the dragonfly.

Had the dogs worn the colour of the hills, had they swung tail round leg, ears oblique and muzzles quivering to scent carrion, or mischief, or the astringency of grouse mingled with the acrid smell of low-clinging sage, the eye might have recognized a congruence between them and the land. Here Coyote, the primitive one, the god-baiter and troublemaker, the thirster after power, the vainglorious, might have walked since the dawn of creation – for Coyote had walked early on the first day.

The dogs, however, were elegant and lithe. They paced with rhythmic dignity. In the downshafts of light their coats shone ebony. The eye observed the fineness of bone, the accuracy of adjustment. As the dogs advanced they gained altitude, circling, until they stood as if freed from the land against the flat blue of the sky.

The eye closed and the dogs sank back into their proper darkness. The eye opened and the dogs stood black against the blue of the iris for the sky was in the eye yet severed from it.

In the light of the eye the dogs could be observed clearly – three Labrador retrievers, gentle, courteous, and playful with the sedate bearing of dogs well schooled to know their worth, to know their place, and to bend willingly to their master's will. One stretched out, face flattened. Its eyes, darker than the grass on which it lay, looked over the rolling hills to the distant saw-tooth pattern of volcanic stone. Behind it the other two sat, tongues dripping red over the saw-tooth pattern of volcanic lip.

The dogs were against the eye and in the eye. They were in the land but not of it. They were of Coyote's house, but become aristocrats in time which had now yielded them up to the timeless hills. They, too, were gods, but civil gods made tractable by use and useless by custom. Here in the hills they would starve or loose themselves in wandering. They were aliens in this spot or exiles returned as if they had never been.

The eye closed. It opened and closed again. Each time the eye opened the dogs circled the hill to the top and trained their gaze on the distant rock. Each time they reached the height of land with more difficulty. At last all three lay pressing thin bellies and jaws against the unyielding earth.

Now when the eye opened there were four dogs and a man and the eye belonged to the man and stared from the hill of his head along the slope of his arm on which the four dogs lay. And the fourth which he had whistled up from his own depths was glossy and fat as the others had been. But this, too, he knew in the end would climb lacklustre as the rest.

So he opened the volcanic ridge of his jaws and bit the tail from each dog and stood with the four tails in his hand and the dogs fawned graciously before him begging decorously for food. And he fed the tail of the first dog to the fourth and the tail of the fourth to the first. In the same way he disposed of the tails of the second and the third. And the dogs sat with their eyes on his mouth.

Then he bit the off-hind leg from each and offered it to the other; then the near-hind leg, and the dogs grew plump and shone in the downlight of his glance. Then the jaw opened and closed on the two forelegs and on the left haunch and the right and each dog bowed and slavered and ate what was offered.

Soon four fanged jaws lay on the hill and before them the man stood rolling the amber eyes in his hands and these he tossed impartially to the waiting jaws. Then he fed the bone of the first jaw to the fourth and that of the second to the third. And taking the two jaws that lay before him he fed tooth to tooth until one tooth remained and this he hid in his own belly.

Afterword

BY GLENN WILLMOTT

Darting in and out of minds, moods, mouths, and eyes like a fish refusing to be caught, Sheila Watson frees herself from storytelling. Or rather, the storytelling we have come to expect is soaked up into something else, into what seems an unfolding, unfurling riddle, whose images, words, and gestures reach down into a human soil too chaotic and fertile with mysteries of myth or madness to grow into stories of the cause-and-effect, one-thing-happened-after-another kind. So her prose feels unreal, and reads more like poetry. The writer Paul Valéry said that while prose merely walks along in straight lines, with an even step, poetry leaps, turns, and pirouettes in a dance. It is easier to understand the movement of Watson's storytelling as this kind of poetry.

Where does this recognition of the stories as akin to poetry take us? A starting point is to begin to wonder, with the bewildered Tolstoy in his *Diaries*, whether just about anything can be poetry, and what poetry really is: "Where the boundary between prose and poetry lies, I shall never be able to understand. The question is raised in manuals of style, yet the answer to it lies beyond me. Poetry is verse: prose is not verse. Or else poetry is everything with the exception of business documents and school books." What makes the question appear even more vexed to us is that poetry of the twentieth century went on to abolish even Tolstoy's exclusion: in the poem "Poetry," Marianne Moore flatly states after listing things to be considered poetic that it is not valid to exclude "business documents and / school-books." Yet, says Moore, when such prosaic things are written by "half poets," it's not necessarily poetry. How to produce it – the real thing, according to Moore, genuine poetry – goes straight to the heart of Watson's poetic style. In "Poetry," Moore says we will have it only when contemporary poets are "literalists of the imagination" able to present "imaginary gardens with real toads in them."

What is a "literalist of the imagination"? In her note of explanation for this first phrase in quotation marks (there is none for the second!), Moore gives us W.B. Yeats's comments on William Blake: "The limitation of his view was from the very intensity of his vision; he was a too literal realist of the imagination, as others are of nature; and because he believed that the figures seen by the mind's eye, when exalted by inspiration, were 'eternal existences,' symbols of divine essences, he hated every grace of style that might obscure their lineaments." So too, Watson does not exclude the reality and experience of madness, or the "imagination," from the reality and experience of "nature." The *poet* as "literalist of the imagination," and *poetry* having "imaginary gardens with real toads in them": this is what Watson and her stories, respectively, offer to us in an unruffled fusion of what is real and what is mythic, what is experienced and what is seen by the mind's eye, or imagined.

After all, Watson grew up within an asylum under the direction of her doctor father, as does the child narrator in "Antigone." Here, she has said, the irrational is rational. Here, madness is the literalizing of imagination, the living out – unselfconsciously, as if fated to do so, "naturally" – of myth: "My father ruled men who thought they were gods or the instruments of gods or, at the very least, god-afflicted and god-pursued. He ruled Atlas who held up the sky, and Hermes who went on endless messages, and Helen who'd been hatched from an egg, and Pan the gardener, and Kallisto the Bear, and too many others to mention by name." It is not merely that these personalities and experiences are affirmed as real, but also as kinds of truth, for Oedipus, Antigone, Daedalus, and other characters outside the asylum also partake of this literalized imagination; it is a peculiar condition that permeates the world, accepted as part of its essence.

What this means when we read the stories is that we do not experience the mythic names as belonging to an allegorical scheme. They do not work together to evoke an imaginative template (for example, the story of Daedalus and Icarus) that we might use to give order and significance to a seemingly messy reality. Rather, Daedalus and other mythic characters are presented as a set of free-floating potentials, tendencies, values, moods, and microplots that can play themselves out authentically – may "literalize" themselves – differently and with degrees of freedom that are only human, in any world in which they unaccountably find themselves. That world is no longer classical Greece, or some pre-contact land of the Shuswaps, but modern Canada. An initial way of finding our way through that world, of mapping it out, might be to ask why some figures, like Oedipus and his family, are able to exist freely in the world, while others, like Helen and Atlas in "Antigone," must be "delivered bound" and "watched over" like "dethroned Titans so that they wouldn't bother Hellas again." Another clue to the organization of this world may be found in the unexpected "fates" of these figures, as opposed to their namesakes of antiquity: why does Atlas "forget the sky" to eat the earth beneath him, or what does Oedipus' new family drama – setting wife against mother, rather than son against father – mean? Moreover, we are asked to consider classical myth simultaneously with other kinds of folk and legend. Oedipus is also the folk trickster, Puss in Boots. Kallisto is also the Northwest Coast hereditary figure, Bear Mother. (In Ovid's *Metamorphoses*, Kallisto is a maiden who arouses both the lust of Jove and the ire of Juno; the latter results in her being transformed into a bear.) Not only are myths "alive" to rewrite themselves in new worlds, they are permeable by other such myths.

What this means practically is that the reader need not struggle to bend characters or story to mythic allusions. The myths themselves are bending, blending, and growing. In good modernist spirit, we are called upon to participate in what these myths mean, not to feel constrained by them, to be with difficulty consumed. We must cultivate these stories as if they were a farm or a garden, which is where Watson's stories generally place us. We approach her garden of symbols, then, as co-creators, with Pan and Oedipus. We put elements together; we place growing things side by side, in sun or shade. To be sure, we may first believe the stories to be constructed of fragmentary puzzle pieces of dialogue, image, and gesture. But the task of gluing such fragments together – as we might in Ezra Pound's *Cantos*, for instance – here defeats us. Hence we learn that what we have are not fragments at all; they are not puzzle pieces whose meaning refers back to a given, allegorical whole, but seeds or genes which mix together in a new, fertile context. The mix and the structure is determined by each story, while the cultivation of particular meaning – what one "finds" in the story – is left to the reader. We are invited to enjoy an intellectual play in the stories, which as Stephen Scobie observes ("Sheila Watson," *Canadian Writers and Their Works*, 1985), is generated out of a shifting, free-ranging, self-ironizing wit. For example, "Why is Oedipus like Puss in Boots?" would be the wrong question because it seeks a prior abstraction, another kind of allegory or template (whose answer is to be found on a bookshelf); "What are the consequences of Oedipus also being Puss in Boots?" would be more relevant.

As soon as we make this kind of "play" our own, we free ourselves from having to know the source of every allusion, or the intention behind every juxtaposition. What we are looking for does not depend upon reconstruction of a hidden order that would be unintelligible if any parts were missing, but upon an "open-ended explorativeness" that for Scobie marks Watson's postmodernism, and will bear unexpected fruits.

"Mythic references are thus points of departure, not arrival," one of Watson's reviewers, David Ingham, has said (*Canadian Literature* 110). Yet there are things it helps to know. Not because, as this reviewer thought, her words were "lacking in a direct link with the world of experience," but because the converse is true. Ironically, the stories can be too directly linked to a historical experience, rather than afloat in literary allusion and verbal play. It is a problem as times and audiences change, for there are kinds of experiences – including experiences of reading – that are too historically specific to be recognized in later years. For example, I admit that I needed Scobie's essay to tell me that the figure named Pierre in "The Rumble Seat" is popular historian Pierre

Berton, and that the story satirizes his book entitled *The Comfortable Pew*. The almost journalistic topicality of the story – the book sparked heated public debate in its day – is echoed by its setting in a television interview. With knowledge of the book and of Berton's cultural status, which belong to a Canadian cultural experience of the 1960s and 1970s, a basic context is indeed restored to the text.

Another such context, also belonging to a literary culture whose intellectual points of reference have since changed, is the modern fascination with comparative mythology initiated by Sir J.G. Frazer's massive, multi-volume study, *The Golden Bough* (1890-1915). Frazer's work, understood not merely as superstition or folk-tale studies but as the new "anthropology," has "influenced our generation profoundly," says Eliot in his headnote to *The Waste Land* (1922). The latter poem, itself the most influential of the century, Eliot tells us is "indebted in general" to Frazer, especially to the volume *Adonis Attis Osiris*, and "deeply" to Jessie L. Weston. Weston's *From Ritual to Romance* (1920) linked Frazer's Adonis–Attis–Osiris mythology with romance literature, and argued that an archaic "vegetation" mythology, especially rituals and narratives of the alienation of a figure representing "life" in an underworld and his return to revive a sterile "waste land" on earth through the mediation of a hero or magician, subtended and permeated the development of medieval romance. Eliot's poem figures modernity itself as a vast "waste land," and his headnote directs attention to "vegetation ceremonies" described by Frazer and Weston in particular to be recognized in the poem. What thus began as a note to a poem, however, became with the rise in authority of Eliot and the emergence of a lingua franca of "myth" in literature, common currency in literary discourse, a cliché. Both Eliot and Watson allow Christian and non-Christian "myths" to permeate each other, and to partake equally, if obscurely, in the meaning of their work. Both Eliot and Watson transform rather than reproduce archaic "vegetation" myths, and it would help contemporary readers if Eliot's headnote were appended to Watson's stories too, for it makes explicit a now missing context of literary experience.

In particular, it is helpful to recognize this experience as the common ground for a startling range of the stories' motifs: the freeing of waters, the ritual burial, the fish feast, the weeping woman, the absent father, the sterile husband, the earth mother or Magna Mater, the journey to the world of the dead, the garden and the figure of the gardener, and the figure of the doctor. While Eliot seemed inclined to parody such pagan motifs and to transcend their earthly significance, Watson's work never does so. Oedipus' withdrawal to his Hades-rooted willow, Antigone's funeral for a bird, Kallisto's grief and adoration, Daedalus' "govi" pots, and Coyote's reversal of the multiplication of life are all grasped as terribly authentic and profound, even through the veil of irony that persistently distances us from any allegorical closure of meaning, from saying this is what is right, that is what is wrong, that is what Watson meant to say. Watson's narrative voice is irreducibly multiple: we side with everyone in turn, including with various animals, and even trees and flowers! As against Eliot's more ascetic vision, the sensual forms and welter of nature, and of desire, are never sacrificed to meaning and order without a sense of unjustifiable loss, hence too without the incorrigible defiance of an Antigone or the incurable madness of a Kallisto.

Eliot refers to "ceremonies" in his poem, and Weston's book finds the origin of literary romance in religious rituals. Our comparative-mythology context reminds us, then, that liturgical or ritual drama – something we may think of as outside the literary – may provide the basis for literary form. And our initial rethinking of the stories as "poetic" should perhaps be revised, to consider the multiplicity of personae (we may think of masks) as dramatic, and their apparently non-narrative actions as ritual. "'The world,' shouted Puss, 'is a vast amphitheatre. We are all actors in a rite.'" Poetry may be the effect, not the cause of the stories' juxtapositional logic and minimal action, which seem to owe more to the dialogic strophe-antistrophe form of classical drama and to the highly condensed, symbolic organization of voice, action, and setting on stage and in ritual ceremony generally.

A final note may be useful as a starting point for thinking about the conflation of Oedipus and Adonis figures. This is the connection between Oedipus and Orpheus in

Watson's mind, which may tacitly subtend these stories. Having completed the other Oedipus stories, she once planned to write a story in which an Orpheus character is "infected" by Oedipus' "stronger mind," catching his "madness at second-hand." The Oedipus–Orpheus connection, however, is already established by Watson's imagination of Oedipus as a poet with underworld associations. (Moreover, the lover's journey to Hades is already worked out via Haemon and Antigone.) The "problem" that motivated the planned story was that "Eurydice comes alive too," and is the "ground in which the [mad] ideas take root to destruction." The missing experiential context, in this case, is not the unwritten story, but the French writer Jean Cocteau's film *Orpheus* (1950), in which the very same problem is worked out. Here the poet is mad, draws his poetry from a parallel world ruled by death, cannot acknowledge his wife, Eurydice, or the imminent birth of their child, and destroys her (and the child), before using his familiarity with the underworld to restore them. Thus Cocteau merges Orpheus, a poet, with an Adonis figure of "life," and works out the problem of the sterile "waste land" in the figure of the alienated wife and denied child. The world of the "waste land" is grasped here as the world of the estranged, unrecognized, or misrecognized family. This context should suggest to us why the family relations of Cocteau's Orpheus appear to displace those of Sophocles' Oedipus in "Brother Oedipus," while

Oedipus' name remains to direct our attention to them.

"Rough Answer," the earliest written of the stories, does not pose the same difficulties of formal coherence and accessibility as the others. Yet in it the reader will recognize the seeds of nearly everything that follows, formally and thematically: voices and minds in counterpoint, revolving points of view, relationships between sensuality and estrangement, and between silence and desire, and destinies that unfold together with those of animal spirits. The coyote that calls Margaret "back to life" yet howls unheard at the end of "Rough Answer" is no doubt akin to the dog whose tooth remains unseen in the man at the end of "And the four animals."

"Rough Answer" was written between 1936 and 1938, the year in which it was published in the September issue of *Canadian Forum*. Undated, but possibly written as early as this, was "The Black Dogs," published under the title "And the four animals" in May 1980 by Coach House Press. "Brother Oedipus," written between 1949 and 1953, was published in the summer number of *Queen's Quarterly* in 1954. "Antigone," initially written in Calgary in 1953 under the title "The Funeral" (Watson also considered two other titles, "Haemon's Story" and "The Magnolia Tree"), was published in the spring number of *The Tamarack Review* in 1959. "The Black Farm," likely written after "Antigone," between 1953 and 1954, was published in *Queen's Quarterly* in the summer of 1956. And "The Rumble Seat" was published in 1974 in *Open Letter*. These six stories represent the complete short fiction published by Sheila Watson.

Apart from her two novels, *The Double Hook* (1959) and *Deep Hollow Creek* (1992), Watson also published a poem, "The Barren Lands," in the October 1934 issue of *Canadian Forum*, and English translations of two stories in French by Madeleine Ferron in Philip Stratford's edition of *Stories from Québec* (1974).

BY SHEILA WATSON

ESSAYS
Sheila Watson: A Collection [*Open Letter*, series 3,
number 1] (Winter, 1974–75)

FICTION
The Double Hook (1959)
Four Stories (1979)
Five Stories (1984)
Deep Hollow Creek (1992)
A Father's Kingdom: The Complete Short Fiction (2004)

The New Canadian Library
The Best of Canadian Writing

Also by Sheila Watson

Deep Hollow Creek
Afterword by Jane Urquhart

When Stella, fresh from her life in the city, arrives to take up her first teaching post in the one-room schoolhouse in a little frontier settlement in the British Columbia interior, she soon finds herself immersed in the stories she is told. Although an outsider in their midst, she sees that for those who dwell in this tiny community, life follows its destined course amid conditions of extraordinary Depression-era hardship.

Written in the 1930s, after Sheila Watson went to the Cariboo country of British Columbia to teach, *Deep Hollow Creek* provides more than a fascinating portrait of a time, a place, and a community. In it, the past resonates with elements of life and human nature that are true for all time.

The Double Hook
Afterword by F.T. Flahiff

doesn't know you can't catch glory on a hook and hold on to it. That ou fish for the glory, you catch the darkness too. That if you hook glory you hook twice the fear. . . ."

llusive prose, Sheila Watson charts the destiny of a small, ommunity nestled in the British Columbia interior. Here, lls of Cariboo country, men and women are caught upon ouble hook of existence, unaware that the flight from danger and he search for glory are both part of the same journey. In Watson's compelling novel, cruelty and kindness, betrayal and faith, shape a pattern of enduring human significance.

NCL A series worth collecting